D0579641

For Julian and Grant... Fly!
BG

Visit us on the web at www.clavisbooks.com

The Only Way I Can written by Bonnie Grubman and illustrated by Carolien Westermann

ISBN 978-1-60537-339-3

This book was printed in December 2016 at Publikum d.o.o., Slavka Rodica 6, Belgrade, Serbia

First Edition
10 9 8 7 6 5 4 3 2 1

Bonnie Grubman & Carolien Westermann

The Only Way I Can

Clavis
NEW YORK

Rabbit gazed up at the graceful bird.
"Yoo-hoo," he called. "How do you do that?"
"Do what?" asked Bird.
"Fly with such ease."
"I was meant to," he said. "I was born to soar the skies."

"I wish I could fly," said Rabbit.
"Really? Where would you go if you could?"
"Into the sunset. Will you help me?"

Bird came down and sized up Rabbit.
"Hmm," he murmured and stroked his chin.
"What do you think?" asked Rabbit eagerly.
I think it's crazy, Bird thought to himself.

"Can you stand on your hind legs and do this?"
asked Bird while spreading his wings.

"Good," he said when Rabbit copied him.
"Now flap like a chicken."
"For how long?"
"Until you achieve lift."

Rabbit flapped until he was standing in a pool of sweat.
"It's not working," he said.
"I can see that," said Bird.
"You'll need to pump up your muscles."

So after twenty or so push-ups
Rabbit tried again.
His feet didn't budge a tiny bit.

"Now what?" asked Rabbit.
"Don't move," said Bird.
Rabbit watched Bird fly into the air in one smooth motion
and land on a branch.
"What are you doing?" Rabbit asked.
"Collecting odds and ends to make a set of wings,"
Bird answered.
"Cool," said Rabbit.

Bird went back and forth until he had everything he needed.
He added some of his own feathers and attached everything to Rabbit.

"How do I look?"
asked Rabbit.
"Pretty funny!
But with any luck,
we'll have you airborne
in no time."

Rabbit spread his makeshift wings. “Perfect,” said Bird. “Now flap like a hummingbird.” Rabbit fluttered his wings forty-eight times per second.

"It's not working," Rabbit panted.
"I can see that. Then it's time
to power-up like a champ."

So he tried more training exercises:

pushups

arm exercises

squats

and even sit-ups,
for some reason.

Then Rabbit ran into the stiff wind….
It didn’t matter.
His feet never left the ground.

"What do we do now?' asked Rabbit.
"Drop a few pounds?" suggested Bird.
Rabbit caught his reflection in the lake.
"Not a chance," he said.
"Then I'm sorry to say I'm fresh out of ideas," said Bird.

"Well, I've got one," said Rabbit.
"But I'll need to go where the eagles soar."
"Now that's a hare-brained scheme if ever I heard one," said Bird.

“Thank you for your kindness,”
Rabbit said and he headed to the cliff.

Bird hovered over Rabbit
and marvelled at his mighty legs.
"Are you sure you want to do this?" shouted Bird.
Rabbit breathed the glorious air
and listened to the breeze
blowing gently through the trees.

"Do what?" asked Rabbit,
his eyes fixed on the changing sky.
"Dive from such a height,
just to try and soar like an eagle?"
"DIVE! Are you cuckoo?
Flying is for birds."

Rabbit lay his furry head on the lush, sweet earth.
He relaxed his long ears and rested his bunny legs.
"Ahh," he said.
"What are you doing?" asked Bird.
"Flying into the sunset the only way I can.
Isn't it beautiful?"
"Magnificent," said Bird.

Rabbit and Bird stared at the spectacular orange glow
that painted the heavens. They stayed there
until the sun took its last peek over the horizon.

When night fell, Rabbit waved good-bye. He took off into the open field and plunged into a hole in the ground.

"Hey down there! How do you do that?" called Bird.
"Do what?"
"Run so fast," Bird answered.
"Oh that," Rabbit said. "I was meant to.
I was born to run with speed and hop into burrows."
Amazing, thought Bird.

Then Bird flew home to his cozy nest…
before he got any crazy ideas.